Bedtime Ba-a-a-lk

Story by Rukhsana Khan
Illustrated by Kristi Frost

Stoddart
Kids
TORONTO • NEW YORK

For Raza, Sophia and Bushra,
my fellow flock-mates.
— R.K.

For Alisa, Lois and Richard,
my loving and supportive family.
— K.F.

We acknowledge the Canada Council for the Arts and the
Ontario Arts Council for their support of our publishing program.

Published in Canada in 1998 by
Stoddart Kids,
a division of Stoddart Publishing Co. Limited
34 Lesmill Road
Toronto, Canada M3B 2T6
Tel (416) 445-3333 Fax (416) 445-5967
E-mail Customer.Service@ccmailgw.genpub.com

Distributed in Canada by
General Distribution Services
30 Lesmill Road
Toronto, Canada M3B 2T6
Tel (416) 445-3333 Fax (416) 445-5967
E-mail Customer.Service@ccmailgw.genpub.com

Published in the United States in 1998 by
Stoddart Kids
a division of Stoddart Publishing Co. Limited
180 Varick Street, 9th Floor
New York, New York 14207
Toll free 1-800-805-1083
E-mail gdsinc@genpub.com

Distributed in the United States by
General Distribution Services
85 River Rock Drive, Suite 202
Buffalo, New York 14207
Toll free 1-800-805-1083
E-mail gdsinc@genpub.com

Canadian Cataloguing in Publication Data

Khan, Rukhsana
Bedtime ba-a-a-lk

ISBN 0-7737-3068-0

I. Frost, Kristi.   II. Title.

PS8571.H37B42 1998   jC813'54   C97-931858-0
PZ7.K42Be 1998

Printed and bound in Hong Kong, China by
Book Art Inc. Toronto

Night has fallen.
Time for gently aching limbs to rest.
A melody of yawns.
And it's upstairs to bed.

Clean teeth.
Tucked in.
Time for sheep to take lullaby leaps.

Conjured visions.
Conjured sheep.
Conjured fence.

"Leap, sheep. Please?"

But a ram, chatting with his flock-mates,
looks at me with forehead furrowed.

"Leap, sheep. Leap."

"Why should we," he asks. "What's in store?
It's dark on the far side of the fence.
Light it up so we can see where we go."

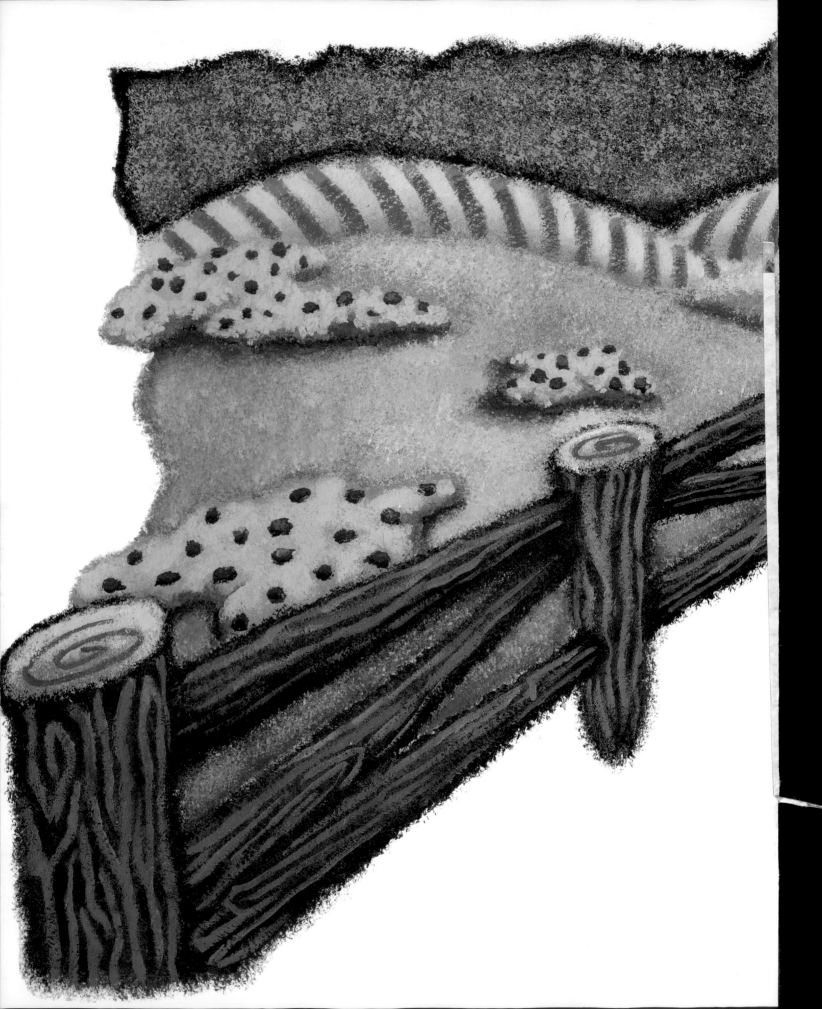

Too tired to argue, I do as he commands.
And conjure a meadow with clover and
buttercups thrown in.

"There, sheep. Will you jump now? Please?
I'd like to count you. I'd like to go to sleep."

The old ram squints
(it seems he's near-sighted), then nods.

"That's a fine meadow. But what about the sky?
Where's the sun? And . . ."

I toss in a sun and quickly color the black sky blue.
But far from being pleased, the old ram looks annoyed.
He speaks a little louder.

"I *was* going to say:
. . . right here where we're standing could use a little work.
It's a wonder we don't fly off into space."

The other sheep murmur agreement.
There's mutiny in the ranks.

A young ewe steps up boldly. "Try to use a little
imagination. That's such a typical meadow.
And that sky is so . . . so . . . ordinary.
You *could* have put in a cloud or two."

But the old ram is cross.
He scolds the ewe for speaking out of turn.
Though he does agree with her.

Exhausted. Why argue?
I fill in the blackness with grass
and, on a whim, toss in a merry-go-round
and Ferris wheel,
hoping that will amuse them.

It does. All too well.
No more grumbling. No arguments.
The sheep have mounted the merry-go-round ponies
and placed their woolly behinds on the Ferris wheel seats.

They squeal with delight as the horses go by
and giggle and laugh when their hooves touch the sky.

They've lost all interest
in jumping the fence.
I call them and call them,
trying hard to be patient.
They don't seem to hear,
and some clearly ignore me.

So I yell, "Stop!"

Even that does no good. They cannot hear me.
I am drowned out by carnival music and roller coasters.
Vendors, calling out, crying out, selling cotton candy.
And helium balloons, caramel corn, and stuffed polar bears.
Baseball caps and candy apples.

Where did they come from? *I* didn't put them there.

I try to be reasonable. "Sheep, please listen," I say.

They choose not to,
not even glancing my way.
Then, as one, their backs turn. A deliberate snub.
They continue to play.

So I do something cruel. Some might even say heartless.
While the sheep are still riding and playing and eating,
I vanish the Ferris wheel, the merry-go-round, the candy.
And everything else, too. The sheep land *thump!*
On their backsides. In blackness. Blinking stupidly.

"JUMP OVER THE DARN FENCE!" I command.

Slowly the old ram gets to his feet,
then rears up on his haunches.
"Who do you think you are, ordering us around!" he says.

Heads nod in back of him. Murmurs of agreement.
"Give her a piece of your mind," bleats the young ewe.

But I stop them before one more word can be uttered.

"Listen, sheep. If you don't do what I say,
I can make more sheep who will obey and be good.
Who will jump over my fence and do as they're told."

A storm gathers across the ram's fluffy, white brow,
and every one of the sheep are standing now. He starts.

"YOU TRULY ARE ONE OF A KIND.
IF YOU THINK WE'RE JUMPING
THAT RICKETY OLD FENCE,
YOU MUST BE OUT OF YOUR . . ."

Gone. All gone. I warned him.
I nestle deeper, cradled in my quilt of eider down.
Toes curled. Soft sheets.
Ready to sleep.

Conjured visions.
Conjured sheep.
Conjured fence.

"Leap, sheep. Leap."

One sheep . . . two sheep . . .
three sheep . . . four.

A few look back over their shoulders,
but say not one word more.